W9-CEH-113

LaSalle Academy Media Center

CYNTHIA RYLANT

The

Heavenly

Village

SCHOLASTIC SIGNATURE

AN IMPRINT OF
SCHOLASTIC INC.

NEW YORK TORONTO LONDON AUCKLAND SYDNEY
MEXICO CITY NEW DELHI HONG KONG BUENOS AIRES

No part of this publication may be reproduced in whole or in part, or stored in a retrieval system, or transmitted in any form or by any means, electronic, mechanical, photocopying, recording, or otherwise, without written permission of the publisher. For information regarding permission, write to Scholastic Inc., Attention: Permissions Department, 557 Broadway, New York, NY 10012.

This book was originally published in hardcover by the Blue Sky Press in 1999.

ISBN 0-439-23149-3

12 11 10 9 8 7 6 5 4 3 2 1   2 3 4 5 6 7/0

Printed in the U.S.A.   40

First Scholastic Trade paperback printing, August 2002

Designed by Kathleen Westray

For D and N

with love

And I saw a new heaven

and a new earth.

REVELATION 21:1

*

The

Village

IT IS SAID that when people die, they travel to a place of Perfect Happiness, a place of Complete Ecstasy, a place called Heaven.

And most do. They hear the voices of angels singing and they see the light of God across the sky and they fly as fast as their new wings can carry them to the most beautiful, the most exquisite world imaginable.

Most of them.

But there are some, a few, a handful in the palm of the universe, who are not so sure about it. Not so sure about wings, about traveling, about leaving behind a sink full of dishes or a dog or a cat. Some left the earth when they were right in the middle of something, and it's nagging at them still as they rise up off the planet on their way to God. There are those who never cared much about seeing new places. Those who thought they *were* living in heaven when they were living on earth. Those who never liked to fly.

And it is these reluctant spirits whom God has watched as they have taken one step into heaven and hesitated. As they have looked back far longer than they have looked ahead. And for whom the light of God is not everything after all.

God calls them His homebodies.

And because He is God and will provide all that anyone ever needs on earth and in heaven, God has made for His homebodies a special stopping place, a wayside, a small pull-over on the way to Perfect Happiness.

It is called The Heavenly Village.

And here these reluctant spirits live, dressed once more in their earthly bodies, half a heart in heaven and half a heart on earth.

They keep a nice little town. Things are always changing. People come and go. Messages fly. Something or someone is always being mended.

The Heavenly Village is filled with angels who have chosen comfortable shoes over wings and who prefer the sound of a teapot to celestial song. They all want to finish something before they travel further, before they accept their Perfect Happiness.

They all want to finish their stories.

And God called the light Day,

and the darkness He called Night.

And there was evening,

and there was morning,

one day.

GENESIS 1 : 5

*

The

Timekeeper

TIME IN the Heavenly Village is a little odd. Just as the spirits who dwell there, it is both part of earth and part of heaven. The Village spirits wouldn't know what to do with themselves if they couldn't have their toast in the morning and their milk at night. They need their lunch hour and bedtime and

Saturdays for errands, otherwise how could they be happy? These are spirits who loved the earth's seasons and all its tickings, the dividing of life into morning joys and evening prayers, the falling of snow before spring. The people in the Heavenly Village loved life's measurings on earth. How else might they have had memories or plans?

Of course, God's time isn't measured at all, and most of the angels flying in the universe love this. They understand eternity. If they never saw another clock in their lives, they wouldn't care.

But not the homebodies. They have a clock in every room. And the Village has one in its tower.

And it is here one may find Everett.

Everett is a small, quiet man who can't believe he has found himself living in the Heavenly Village. In fact, he can't believe he has found himself living at all. When he was a man on earth, Everett had no faith in heaven whatsoever. No faith in angels or spirits. No faith in anything except what he could see right in front of him.

And this is most depressing of all, for what Everett could see right in front of him was so uninspiring that one would think Everett would have wished for angel's wings every single day of his life.

What Everett saw in front of him, every single day of his life, was money.

Everett was a bank teller.

Of course, being a bank teller is a perfectly fine occupation provided the teller likes helping people take care of their finances, likes smiling at the next person at the window, takes a certain pride in counting out all that money day after day and never making a mistake or dropping all the quarters.

There isn't a thing wrong with being a bank teller. And Everett was actually pretty good at it.

It's just that, after a while, Everett forgot

to stop counting. He would count ones and tens and twenties all day long at the bank, then go home and count how many forks he had. He counted his socks and his shirts and his ties. He counted his lightbulbs (twice — those in the lamps and those in the pantry). He counted out cans of soup and slices of bread and spice bottles.

And all of this, slightly strange as it was, would have been all right except for one thing:

Everett started counting beauty.

He didn't know when it happened, when the first day was that he stopped in front of a spider's web and counted off each and every glistening strand, or when he looked up at a flock of white snow geese flying overhead and counted the birds out in sections of six, or when he stood beside the sea and calculated the number of seconds between waves.

But somehow, in the passing of time, Everett completely forgot that a thing could simply be *beautiful*. He thought only of the mathematics. Is it any wonder, then, that he lost faith in heaven?

Everett was forty-six years old when he died. Something went wrong with his heart. Imagine his surprise when, after a life devoid of faith and beauty, Everett found himself floating to heaven.

The journey from earth to heaven can be long or short, depending on how much thinking God feels one ought to do. For Everett, He allowed a little extra time.

And as Everett floated through that lovely yellow light toward heaven, guess what he saw:

A spider's web.

It was so exquisite that Everett nearly wept. He didn't think once about counting.

He saw a flock of white snow geese above him and he ached with joy.

Then he found himself floating beside a silvery blue sea. A wave rolled in to shore and

Everett put his fingers into the warm white foam and tasted them. And as he looked out at the large white moon shining softly and steadily over the water, Everett wished he had a second chance.

That is when he found himself sitting on a park bench in the Heavenly Village.

Everett looked down and saw that he was wearing his own clothes and his own shoes and even his silver wristwatch with the flexible band. He was forty-six, intact, and for a moment he thought he hadn't died after all.

Until an elderly woman in a gardener's smock and a straw hat appeared beside him and said, "Welcome to the Heavenly Village."

Everett raised his eyebrows.

"So I'm dead after all?" he asked.

"Heavens, no," said the woman. "No one dies. They just relocate."

Everett looked around him. There was a village green with a small white church and a clock tower. There was a street of small shops. There was a boy on a skateboard and a dog running beside him. Someone was pruning a tree in the small park. And several people rode past on bicycles.

"Is this Connecticut?" asked Everett.

The elderly woman smiled.

"It is not quite earth and not quite heaven," she said. "It is a halfway place for undecided angels."

She held out her hand.

"I'm Doris," she said.

"Everett," said Everett, shaking her hand. "Pleased to meet you."

"Let me take you home now," said Doris.

And suddenly Everett found himself in a clean little apartment above the Village bakery.

"Oh, it smells wonderful here," he said.

Doris smiled.

"Already you are changing."

"Pardon me?" asked Everett.

"Never mind," said Doris. "Let me help you settle in."

And Doris helped Everett settle in. He loved his little apartment:

"A blue bedroom — perfect!"

"Oh, look at the view from *this* window!"

"Doris, did someone refinish this old dresser by hand?"

Doris just smiled.

Doris then took Everett to the grocery store for a few things, and when they returned, she told him finally why he had been placed in the Heavenly Village.

"You will be our new Timekeeper, Everett, for our old one has moved on."

"A Timekeeper?" asked Everett.

"Yes," said Doris. "The clock in the Village tower must be wound each morning and each evening. Its chimes must ring at noon. And the mainspring needs oiling now and then."

"That's all?" asked Everett. "That's all I have to do?"

Doris put on her straw hat and headed toward the door. She smiled one last time.

"It is enough," she said. And then she was gone. (Doris didn't disappear. She just walked down the hall like anybody else. The Village spirits are not really interested in impressing newcomers with their ability to project themselves anywhere in the universe in a millisecond. They're really much more interested in what good books one has read lately.)

So that is how Everett became the Village Timekeeper, and in the Village tower is where he is now.

Everett, of course, is something of an exception in the Heavenly Village. Given the complete lack of appreciation he had had for the earth's beauties, one would think Everett wouldn't qualify for Village life at all. Those in the Village love the earth and all its small things.

But the Village must have a Timekeeper, and it must be someone who won't be distracted with making a carrot cake, or painting a landscape, or building a nice stone wall around one's garden. The clock in the Village tower is the most important piece of equipment in town, for it measures out earth time in God's heaven, and without it, the spirits in the Village would be completely confused about what was going on on the earth.

Without a clock to tell what time it is or a calendar to tell what year it is, a villager might think her grandchild was just about to be born when in fact it had already happened three thousand years ago. (In God's heaven, there is not much difference between right now and three thousand years ago.) Another villager planning a trip to the kite festival in Astoria, Oregon, could arrive two million days too late.

The correct time is essential for the

villagers, for nothing is more important to them than being perfectly connected to the earth. It is this connection that will help them finish their stories.

So the clock has to be right. And Everett is just the person to keep it that way. The counting off of earthly minutes, days, and years will be, for Everett, a cinch.

But keeping earth's time isn't the real reason God has placed Everett in the Heavenly Village. God knows that there are plenty of people who can do a Timekeeper's job.

God has put Everett here because Everett asked for a second chance.

Everett wants to know something of beauty. And here God will give him what his heart desires.

So each morning when Everett opens his eyes he will listen through his window to the sound of a wind chime singing softly in the tree outside. He will feel the soft fur of his cat Penelope's face against his hand. He will smell the bread baking below. And he will lie a moment or two extra, appreciating these things.

Then Everett will rise up from his bed and walk to the clock tower. He will wave to the boy on the bike delivering the Village paper. He will marvel at the fog hanging low over the lamplights. He will search for the tips of sunrise on the mountains.

At the tower Everett will climb carefully up to the clock and he will begin to wind it so that twelve earthly hours will tick away. And as he winds each of the twelve hours, Everett will spend twelve moments on earth.

Winding the first hour, he will see a young mother and her baby in a bus station. The mother is overwhelmed. Too young, too broke, too lonely. And Everett will shine an invisible light on her baby's small head, causing its fair hair to glow like the sun. And the young mother will catch this beauty and be restored.

When he winds the second hour, Everett will see a classroom of children. Their teacher has forgotten that each child is a heavenly spirit. She hasn't seen the light inside them for a long time. Everett will remind her.

And with each and every hour, Everett will visit someone on earth, reminding that person of its beauty.

Then when he is finished, he will walk home through the Village, pick up Penelope, and head to the park to read.

Thou shalt take fine flour,

and bake twelve cakes

thereof.

LEVITICUS 24:5

The

Baker

ALL OF the spirits in the Heavenly Village have their dear little routines, and these routines have much to do with who the spirits were on earth. In the small yellow house on the corner of Sycamore and Oak (the Village streets all have comforting earthly names), there is a young girl who practices piano every day at four o'clock. She does this because her mother always told her to, and living in the Heavenly Village makes one especially good about doing things one ought. There is a boy who keeps everyone's lawns mowed. There is a man who fills all the bird feeders. There is a sweet old grandmother who bakes everyone a pie.

And there is also another baker in the Village. Her name is Violet Rose.

Violet Rose is a lovely young woman, and her name suits her. She seems like a flower. She wears wispy skirts and silk blouses and shoes embroidered in China. Her hands are small and delicate and her skin light and pink. Violet Rose's house is decorated with large old-fashioned mirrors and Indian scarves and lamps with rose-colored shades. And she is in the Heavenly Village because of her cats. Violet Rose is waiting for them.

Most people who pass on into God's heaven are able to leave behind such things as cats and dogs and pet birds without much worry, for once they have seen God's light, they understand in a way they were never able to on earth that *all is well*. They believe in forever and they know that those they love on earth will soon be with them. Everything is all right.

Violet Rose, however, is not one of those people. God knew that right away.

On earth, Violet Rose had had a very sad childhood. This is always something God has little power over. (And because of this, He sometimes has a lot of explaining to do to the new arrival in heaven.)

But God could not make Violet Rose's parents loving people, and He could not give Violet Rose a peaceful, quiet home, and He could not keep her tears from flowing.

He did what He could: He made white daisies grow outside her bedroom all summer long, and He sent a bright red cardinal to live in her snowy yard each winter, and He turned the moon a certain way each night so its light would shine upon her as she slept.

But though all of these things helped a little, none of them would ever convince Violet Rose that all was well. Because, for her, it wasn't.

And so she grew up always a bit worried, a bit fearful. She was always afraid that anything nice that came into her life might suddenly go away.

Once Violet Rose was old enough, she left her parents' unhappy house and she struck out on her own. She took a bus to California and she lived in a little room in a boardinghouse and she got a job as a waitress at a vegetarian restaurant.

And it was here that Violet Rose learned to bake bread. The restaurant's usual bread-baker moved away, and the owner asked Violet Rose if she might want the job. She decided to give it a try.

For someone who has grown up in an

unpeaceful house, baking bread in the soft dark hours of morning is the most wonderful, most peaceful experience on earth. Violet Rose awoke at 4 A.M. every day and walked the few blocks to the restaurant in sheer happiness, and as she pulled open the old screen door that led to the restaurant's rear kitchen, she sometimes said, to whomever might be listening, "Thank you."

Well, someone was listening. God always listened to Violet Rose. And though the only things He could take credit for were the bread and the dawn, He was always pleased when she expressed her gratitude.

Violet Rose saved just enough money baking bread that eventually she was able to rent her own little apartment. It was on the second floor of a large old house near the restaurant, and it had a small fireplace and a built-in china hutch and even a tiny balcony. Violet Rose loved it. Here is where she learned to decorate with scarves.

And here is where she found her cats.

It is probably more accurate to say that here is where the cats found *her*, for Violet Rose never had to go out searching the world for a cat. Every so often, when she opened her front door, one was just sitting there.

Oliver arrived first. He had several bites on his ear and his left eye was swollen shut and he was so tired he didn't even bother to meow that first day.

Violet Rose just picked him up and carried him in and he became hers.

Next was Edgar. Edgar was a beautiful white cat but no one could see this for all the dirt and grime. It was anyone's guess where Edgar had been living.

He let Violet Rose carry him in, too.

Claude arrived in the rain and five pounds too skinny.

Marsh arrived at ten below zero, with icicle whiskers.

And Jackson just showed up in the kitchen

one morning. Violet Rose didn't know how he got in. But she let him stay.

Five tomcats living with Violet Rose. Five tomcats and not one hiss, not one swat, not one bite. Pure cat bliss.

Imagine how this changed Violet Rose. How living with peaceful, loving creatures changed her. Then imagine how disappointed she was when she died.

Violet Rose was hit by a car on her way to bake bread one morning. The man driving the car never stopped. And as her spirit body was rising up from her earthly body to live in God's heaven, Violet Rose steered herself around and back toward her little apartment. She went inside and petted the head of each of her five tomcats sleeping on the bed, then she left the earth for good.

Violet Rose looked back with worry at those sleeping cats a hundred times on her way to heaven's door. God didn't even try having an angel talk her into flying out into the universe. He just let her fly straight to the Heavenly Village, into the little house where she lives now.

So Violet Rose is baking bread in the Heavenly Village while she waits for her cats.

Now here is where the subject of time comes up again. For had Violet Rose chosen to fly on into God's universe when she died — instead of stopping at the Heavenly Village and buckling on her Chinese shoes — she could have been with her cats again in the blink of an eye. Because in God's universe, time moves as slow or fast, as backward or forward, as anyone wants it to. In God's universe, Violet Rose could have been with her cats in an instant, because although in earth time the cats had probably ten or twelve more years to live, in God's time they had only the tiniest bit of a blink. They would have been there right behind her, if Violet Rose had flown on into heaven.

But instead she chose earth time and a life in the Village. Why? Because she knew, without God even having to tell her, that becoming an angel just so she could be with her cats again was not the best reason. A person has to really want those wings. Violet Rose knows she isn't ready. She appreciates God and His goodness and she's glad He has a universe of angels.

She just doesn't want to be one of them. Not yet. Claude has a strange little bump on his toe and Edgar's allergies are acting up and Marsh needs a tonic.

She's not ready.

The cats are all actually doing quite well. The woman who rented the apartment to Violet Rose was so brokenhearted when the young girl died that she decided to keep all the cats herself and let them stay in the apartment. The woman lives downstairs so it's easy for her to check up on them. She leaves the back bedroom window slightly open, so they can come and go.

The cats are all right. They have each other. And cats are not the worriers most people are. They seem to understand they'll see Violet Rose again. Any second now.

The landlady is not the only person who is sad about Violet Rose. The man who owned the restaurant was also heartbroken. He had someone paint a picture of a vase holding a single violet and a single rose, and he hung the picture beside the restaurant's front door.

Violet Rose is so surprised by all this. She didn't know, really, that people cared about her.

It makes her happy.

Violet Rose's bread-baking has become quite extraordinary since she moved to the Village. There is just something about heavenly flour. And Violet Rose doesn't cut corners on time, either. People in the Village know that they can tap into universe time if ever they want to. It is a sort of Village convenience. If a person wants something to happen in five minutes instead of waiting two weeks, he can make it so. It isn't, as they say in the Village, "kosher," but it can be done.

Violet Rose doesn't really have to wait two hours for her bread to rise. She could make it happen in a split second, using universe time.

But Violet Rose is a true baker. She loves the slow rise.

So she spends each day baking the Village her bread, and she leaves it at the bakery for anyone who wants it. The man who owns the bakery specializes in dinner rolls, so he's happy to have the loaves. And the Village electrician says he even thinks Violet Rose's bread will make his hair grow back. (He is bald. The Heavenly Village doesn't fix everything.)

And every few days, Violet Rose sends her spirit body back to earth to visit her cats, and anyone there who notices small events would know this. Edgar stops his scratching. Oliver purrs twice as loud. Marsh licks Claude's face. Jackson shares his food.

And all is well.

For this is the message

which we have heard

from the beginning,

that we should love

one another.

1 JOHN 3:11

*

The Boy

and the Dog

THE LIFE of a child in the Heavenly Village is not much different from the life of a child on earth, except that in the Heavenly Village, children are rather rare. Most children who die fly straight to heaven so fast, even God Himself is sometimes surprised by how soon they get there. Children have not lived on earth long enough to be deeply sentimental about it. They like their parents, their friends, their toys and their pets. But because they haven't been long on earth, they are still more spirit than human, and they know exactly what they want to do when they rise up from the planet. They want to fly faster than light straight back to the heaven where they came from and play like puppies. Children like the earth, but they *adore* heaven.

So it is a little unusual for a child to want to stop in the Heavenly Village and stay. Why would he want a bed he has to make and homework he has to do when he could be zipping all over the universe having heaven-knows-what kind of fun?

Because someone he has traveled to heaven with isn't ready for the universe. Someone he knows — and loves — can't move on.

And that is why the people in the Village see a lot of Harold and his dog.

Harold's dog is named Fortune because the man who gave the dog to Harold — when Harold was eight years old and still on earth — said, "This dog is worth a fortune, but you can have him for free." Harold had been standing on a street corner, waiting for the light to change, when the man came up to him, spoke those words, then handed him the dog's leash and walked away.

Harold, of course, did what any boy would do. He took the dog home.

And it turned out that the man's words actually *were* true: Fortune revealed himself to be an amazingly intelligent, heroic, *legendary* dog. Fortune became a rescue dog.

Most rescue dogs require special training. They have special handlers who teach them how to track lost children, how to find people after earthquakes and avalanches, how to save someone who is drowning.

No one had to teach Fortune.

The first person Fortune saved was an elderly man caught by the ocean's undertow. Harold and Fortune were walking along the sand when suddenly Fortune tore off, yanking the leash out of Harold's hand, running so fast up the beach that Harold lost sight of him.

Harold couldn't imagine what had made Fortune behave so badly, and he ran in the dog's direction with the words *Bad dog!* ready in his mouth.

But he never said them. Harold found Fortune pulling a frail old man out of the surf, the man clinging to the dog's neck and gasping for air. Then crying and hugging the dog.

That was Fortune's first rescue. There would be more.

He found a kitten who had fallen down a drainpipe. He found a toddler in the woods. He pulled a girl from a burning apartment. He lifted a puppy off a busy highway. He even tracked down an escaped cockatiel.

Fortune loved two things in life: Harold and rescue. And it was both that brought him to the Heavenly Village.

The death of a child is a terrible thing for anyone, but for those with faith in God it can be hardest of all. How could God have let this happen? they ask. Where was He, where were His angels?

It is hard for them to accept that God was watching all along and did let it happen.

And it is true that God saw Harold tip out of the big inner tube he was riding on the river and go under. And it is true that God saw Fortune leap from the riverbank to save Harold, and instead be pulled under by the same impossibly strong current which no creature had hope of swimming against.

It is true that God saw everything. But, of course, Harold and Fortune were practically in His lap within half a moment, so God was not all that troubled by the event. Harold and

Fortune were just fine. Neither had any memory of fear or discomfort at all, and both would have jumped right back in that river for fun if, of course, they hadn't already gone to heaven.

Instead, they did what any boy and dog who go to heaven together would do. They flew off to play.

And at first it seemed Harold and Fortune would do this forever. Until Fortune began trying to rescue angels who didn't need rescuing.

The first angel Fortune rescued was standing in the path of a comet. Fortune pushed him out of the way.

Unfortunately, the angel hadn't wanted to be pushed out of the way. The angel had been *constructing* the comet and had nearly gotten it just perfect, had nearly gotten the tail just right, when Fortune bounced across the sky and pushed him over and knocked out a big chunk of cosmic gas.

Angels are models of forgiveness — or are supposed to be — so the angel told Harold and Fortune never mind. That he could always make another comet.

But Harold could see that, underneath, the angel was a bit miffed. Harold felt bad.

It wasn't long before Fortune tried to save another angel, this time from a falling star. The angel said, *"Thank you anyway, but I didn't need saving,"* and, of course, Harold felt bad again.

Finally, when Fortune tried to save his tenth angel (with disastrous results — it didn't stop snowing in Delaware for *weeks*), God realized this beloved and legendary dog didn't belong in heaven. He belonged in the Heavenly Village.

Fortune had just been trying to finish his story.

So God sent Harold and Fortune to live with a woman in the Village named Eleanor whom they've grown to love very much. Eleanor built a tree house for Harold (she's very handy) and she taught Fortune to go up and down a slicky-slide (which he thinks is a fine trick), and everything is working out very nicely. Harold doesn't mind being a boy a while longer. There were a few things he'd wanted to get back to — including a book on polar bears, which he now has a copy of thanks to another boy who was flying through with it on his way to heaven.

And Harold's dog, Fortune, has reclaimed his legendary status. Already he's rescued a villager from a runaway lawn mower and another who was about to fall off a ladder. He helped Everett the Timekeeper get his foot unstuck from a hole. And if there's ever a lost kitten in the Village, everyone knows whom to call.

For some, work is heaven. Fortune is a happy dog.

I am as a wonder

unto many.

PSALMS 71:7

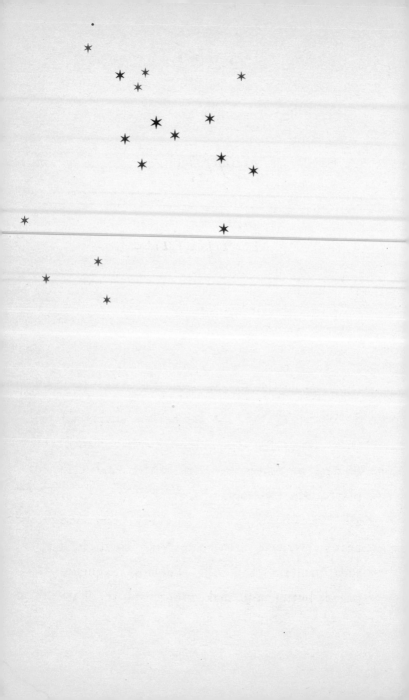

*

The

Magician

THE HEAVENLY VILLAGE contains all those things that make a small town beautiful. A peaceful river flows beside it, and tiny playful birds swoop and loop above the water all day. The lawns are soft and green and nearly everyone grows flowers. There is a soda fountain that sells the most exquisite peanut butter milk shakes. In spring there are rainbows after the storms and in winter just enough snow for a snowman. There is a library filled with the best books ever written and a movie theater with stars on the ceiling. (*It's a Wonderful Life* is always the midnight show.)

But the Village has its oddities, too. Take mail, for example. On earth a person writes a letter, drops it in a box, then waits four or five days for it to arrive. The letter passes through post offices and mail trucks and mail planes and mail carriers until finally it reaches the person it is meant for.

God has been watching all this for years, and He thinks the postal service needs improving. It is simply too slow.

Naturally, He can't interfere with things on earth. But He can do what He likes in heaven.

So God created Thought Mail.

Thought Mail is the way spirits in the Heavenly Village correspond not only with other spirits in the Village but also with people in heaven and on earth. God says that everything important that was ever done probably started with a thought letter. Even holy books like the Bible and the Koran are nothing but collections of some of the best thought letters ever sent from heaven to earth. "In the beginning was the Word, and the Word was with God, and the Word was God." John 1:1. Just a thought an angel had one day that was too good to ignore. He sent it to someone on earth.

Because God has always understood how important ritual is, He tells His angels and villagers that even though the letters are sent telepathically, everyone should use nice stationery. So it's not uncommon to see a villager carrying a small folder of pretty papers and pens and stamps to the park. The villager will write his letter, put it in its envelope, stamp it, and then — because it is Thought Mail — simply send it from his heart.

The letter will disappear somewhere into

the universe, but the words contained in it will float on their own and settle into the mind of the person the letter is intended for. That person may be another villager, who will receive every word provided he isn't in the middle of an exciting book. Or it may be an angel in the universe, who will understand everything perfectly.

Or it may be a person on earth who, because he is probably busy and surrounded by so much noise and distraction, will be lucky if he receives even the first sentence in his mind. Sometimes it takes several thought letters to get through to a person on earth. (God has tried a million ways of getting humans to listen better, like giving them oceans to look at and beautiful night skies to think under and absolutely silent sunrises. But most people ignore all that.)

There are some humans, though, who hear almost nothing *but* thought letters. The magician was one of them.

Magicians on earth were magicians in heaven before they were born, and it is this that drives them nuts. They knew *all* the tricks when they were spirits in heaven.

Every illusion ever performed, every trade secret ever known was available to them when they were angels. And the thing about any magician is that he is always obsessed about the secrets of every other magician. If a magician sees someone make something disappear and he can't figure out how it was done, he will spend the rest of eternity finding out.

So in heaven, magician spirits know everything and they are content. But when these spirits are born on earth, they can't remember any of it. And they spend the rest of their lives trying to get their secrets back.

Isham Taylor was no exception. His mother hit it on the head when she said, "Isham was *born* a magician." Of course he was. And that is why Isham spent all of his childhood trying to figure out how to hide an ace of clubs in a deck, how to pull a quarter from behind some-one's ear, how to turn one scarf into fifty.

Easy stuff.

But Isham had to know *everything*. So as he got older, he studied more serious illusion. Escape from barrels and chains, levitation, making a person disappear into thin air.

Isham woke up each morning with an illusion in his mind and he wouldn't go to bed at night until he'd performed it. Magicians are not really very comfortable on earth, and Isham was *never* comfortable. All he could think about was magic.

All of this thinking is what naturally made him such a good receiver of thought letters. Every magician, artist, composer, writer living in heaven is searching for someone on earth to share some knowledge with. Searching for an open mind and heart.

For the magicians in heaven who had things to tell him, Isham was just one big TV antenna. Thought letters flew to him every day, and he listened carefully to them all. He became famous. Famous and rich and, ultimately, a mess.

Isham turned into a drinker. All of that magic he did every day, the heaviness in his mind caused by thinking and thinking, led him to seek relief. He turned to drink.

After each grand performance in concert halls and auditoriums, Isham would go off by himself into the night. He would drive his big black car around the empty streets of whatever town he was in and he would drink for relief.

And it was when he was driving around one of those little towns at four in the morning that he hit Violet Rose.

The thing about magic that magicians know for sure but that other people are only a little convinced of is that it is all illusion. Nothing a magician does is real. It hasn't really happened. Magicians *fool* people, that's all. They can't really change anything.

Isham couldn't change what he did that night. He hit a young girl. He couldn't bring her back to life. He couldn't make her disappear. So he kept on driving.

Isham never made amends. He not only never confessed, but he never tried, during the rest of his life, to do good works to make up for the bad he'd done. He got richer, more famous, more talented, and he kept drinking. Isham never made amends.

So what does God do with someone like Isham when he dies?

God allows him into heaven.

Again and again God has told His spirits that He is their father. And sometimes She has told them She is their mother. Every spirit in the world is a child of God. Every spirit.

It is easy for the angels in heaven and the villagers in the Village to remember this. But on earth, nearly everyone forgets.

There are earthly reminders: A young man will do a terrible thing, and the whole world will hate him and call him evil. But his father and mother will look at him and say, "I love you."

People on earth forget that God is father and mother.

So when someone like Isham dies, full of wrong deeds, many people think Isham will go to hell.

But he doesn't. He goes home.

When Isham finally died of a stroke in his sleep, eight years after hitting Violet Rose, he lifted up to heaven like everyone else. Everything that comes from God returns to God — including Isham.

And when he arrived, there was God and His angels and all that goodness and love, and Isham, looking back at the terrible life he'd lived on earth, could not bear it. He could not bear the shame, and if ever there was a real hell, it was the burning misery in Isham's heart.

There is no father and mother in the world

who will not forgive a child. No father and mother anywhere.

God forgave Isham. Then He sent Isham to earn the real forgiveness he needed: God sent Isham to Violet Rose.

Isham lives two doors away from Violet Rose. He has become her friend. He brings her tomatoes from his garden and good books he's read. He loans her his favorite records. He brought her a little bird.

Every day Isham watches Violet Rose carry her bread to the bakery and he weeps. He watches her travel to earth to pet her cats and he weeps.

Every day Isham carries a small folder of nice stationery and pens to the park and he tries to write the thought letter he knows he must one day send. He tries to write that letter to Violet Rose, but, so far, he hasn't been able. He cannot bear it. He loves her.

God is with him.

* * *

He that followeth

after righteousness and kindness

findeth life.

PROVERBS 21:21

*

The

Doctor

ONE OF the nicest things about living in the Heavenly Village is that no one ever gets sick. The houses are earth houses, the food is earth food, the flowers are earth flowers. But time is always relative. It is what anyone needs it to be. So if someone wants petunias all year long, she has petunias all year long. If someone loves the beautiful orange leaves of his maple tree in autumn and wants them never to fall off, they won't. And if someone gets a cold or a sore throat or the mumps and doesn't want to keep them (and who would?), the illness is gone in an instant. The person just shifts his molecules two weeks ahead. (This playing around with time still confuses some villagers, and on earth, of course, it kept everyone baffled for centuries until Albert Einstein came along. And even he had trouble explaining it.)

So in a village where no one ever gets sick, why would there be a doctor?

Because the doctor hasn't finished his story.

The doctor's name is Raphael Blake. He died when he was only thirty-four years old, and this was a bit of a shock to him. Not that he died so young, but that he died at all. Doctors never believe they are going to die. Dr. Blake certainly never thought he would. He had a nice practice, a good wife, a wonderful son, and two dogs. And he was a doctor. Dying was the last thing he thought would happen to him. Until the day he was hiking with another doctor and fell off a mountain.

It was when he was falling, and time had slowed almost to a stop, that Dr. Blake finally thought about death. And this part was actually not so hard for him. It was when he thought about life — and realized he loved it — that he tried to stay. That he tried not to die. But he was already falling.

And as he fell, Dr. Blake saw his son.

The child had been born on a beautiful September day seven years before. As he fell, Dr. Blake remembered the roses that day on the hospital lawn. He remembered their smell. He remembered his young wife. And he remembered his baby boy.

The child's name was Jay. When he was born, he hardly cried at all. He smiled. People say that newborns can't smile. But Jay could. He lay in his father's arms and smiled at him.

Dr. Blake saw this as he fell. And he wanted more memories of Jay. He reached out. He wanted other pictures to take with him when he died.

But they weren't there. Dr. Blake was still looking for them when he hit the ground. Still searching when his spirit rose up. Still reaching as he followed the light to heaven.

And he knew, he knew, why he couldn't find any other memories of his son, Jay.

Because Dr. Blake was never home long enough to make a memory good enough to keep.

And this was because he worked.

Dr. Blake worked six days a week from seven o'clock in the morning until eight o'clock at night. When he finally came home, his little boy had already had his supper, read his books, found his bear, and gone to bed.

Dr. Blake never knew what the books had been about nor where the bear had been found nor what sweet things his son might have said before going to sleep.

Because nothing mattered as much to Dr. Blake as his work. And because of this, he missed everything. Everything about his son that was worth knowing. Everything that was precious and temporary. He missed it all.

And when he fell off the mountain, he didn't have anything to take with him.

A heart filled with regret is not ready for the universe. Dr. Blake's spirit body floated up and he saw the luminous wings of angels and felt the love of God all around him and he knew he was at the threshold of heaven.

But all he could say, as he stood there at God's door, was, "My son."

An angel named Margaret led him to the Heavenly Village.

And here he is, a doctor living in a town where no one gets sick.

He has a small doctor's office. It's in a white-frame building with black shutters and sits next to a coffee shop. There's a clean waiting room with light blue commercial carpet and sturdy vinyl chairs and several good magazine subscriptions. Dr. Blake asked if there could be a fish tank, and of course one was installed the same day. God provides.

One might imagine the waiting room would always be empty. But it isn't. Most days there are at least one or two villagers there, waiting to see the doctor.

When he first began seeing villagers in his office, Dr. Blake attended to the usual matters: weight, temperature, blood pressure, peering into the ears and all that.

But, of course, everything was normal. No one was ever sick.

So why do the villagers come to Dr. Blake?

To talk. None of them have ever been to a doctor who actually talked with them. When the villagers heard there was one in town who would, well, they knew for sure they'd died and gone to heaven.

Dr. Blake talks with his patients. He hears about their gardens and their grandchildren and their favorite recipes for chicken. He learns about their hobbies and their passions and their deepest earthly fears. He notices if their eyes are brown or blue, if they are freckled, if their hair is thick or thin. He asks who they were named for. He asks what they like to eat. He compliments their clothing.

And while no one who walks into his office is ever really sick to begin with, every single one of them leaves saying, "I feel so much better."

Dr. Blake loves his work in the Heavenly Village just as he had loved his work on earth.

But here, near God's heaven, he is wiser.

He leaves his office at four o'clock every day and goes home in time for supper. Of course, at his house in the Village, there is no one there. It doesn't matter. That isn't the home he goes to anyway.

He goes to his home on earth. And he sits in the kitchen and speaks to his wife as she prepares spaghetti for supper. She doesn't hear him. But he is there.

And after visiting with his wife, he sits beside his son and watches a cartoon on television and laughs in all the same places with him. He notices how silky his young son's hair is, how smooth his hands, how clear and blue his eyes. He sees inside the boy how God's light is shining, has always been shining there. Will always shine.

Dr. Blake has supper with his family and then reads a book with his wife to their young son. The book is about a sweet dragon. And when the story is finished and the boy has fallen asleep, with his bear in his arms, his father leaves.

God will kindly allow Dr. Blake to practice medicine in the Heavenly Village and to go home in time for supper for as long as he needs.

It may be a while.

My days are swifter

than a weaver's shuttle....

JOB 7:6

✴

The

Runner

THE PEOPLE in the Heavenly Village can be whatever age they want to be, whatever height, whatever weight they choose. Those who always wished they were taller can be so in the Heavenly Village. Those who wanted bigger muscles can have them. If someone just couldn't lose that last five pounds on earth, she can do it in the Heavenly Village — if she chooses.

But — and this was a revelation even to God Himself — most people want to stay just the way they are. This has surprised even the villagers, but it is true. In the Heavenly Village, with no fear of illness or death, with no worry about whether others will find them attractive and good-looking, the spirits finally decide they look just fine. They accept their earthly bodies, and in their spirit wisdom, they eat good food for those bodies. They understand, finally, the teaching "As within, so without." They eat well. But hardly anyone is interested anymore in actual exercise.

And this is why there's almost never anyone on the Village running path except Cordie.

Cordie loves to run.

Her proper name is Cordelia, but that's a

name much too long for someone who moves so fast. On earth her friends call her Cordie.

Cordie was fourteen when she died and she is fourteen still. She is on the Village running path by six o'clock every morning and she is on it again at six o'clock at night. She runs seven miles each time. Everyone in the Village sees her, every day, running.

Some wonder why she cares. They think, "Why doesn't that girl just go to a nice movie and enjoy herself? Why can't she be still?"

But few people, even heavenly spirits, can understand a runner's heart.

Cordie began running when she was four years old. She followed her father to the park and she ran behind him. He ran for exercise. But Cordie ran for love. She loved to run. Before long, she was running in front of him. She was running in front of everyone. People would look at her fly past and say, "That girl is going to be famous someday."

But Cordie never got the chance to be famous. She died young, and quickly, of leukemia. Everyone said it wouldn't happen. They said, "That girl's too strong. She'll outrun that leukemia." But she didn't. Other people in the hospital with leukemia got better. But Cordie died.

And for her, this wasn't bad at all. Because for someone who just can't move fast enough, leaving an earthly body is the most heavenly experience in the world. Cordie floated up out of that heavy old body and she ran like no one has ever run before. She went up into the clouds and she ran faster than sound, faster than light, faster than anyone had ever seen before. Even the angels in heaven stopped for a second to watch her.

"Now there goes a runner's heart," said one. Nearer God, angels receive much of His wisdom.

Cordie had never been able to explain to

people on earth why she so loved to run. She could not explain where it took her, how it changed her. She would run and her heart would fly. That was all she knew.

But when she died, Cordie finally realized how she could have explained it.

"It is like dying," she could have said. But then, of course, *no one* would have understood her.

So when she passed away, Cordie simply ran straight up to God's universe, ready to go in and run some more.

But on her way to heaven, Cordie caught a glimpse of the Heavenly Village. She saw just one thing — those tiny birds playing above the Village river — and she had to stop and stay.

Cordie had almost forgotten the other part of her story.

In Cordie's hometown, there was a young man who kept parrots. He lived in a house near the river, and the running path ran beside this river, so Cordie often heard those parrots through the open windows, talking and squawking and entertaining the young man day after day.

Then, after a time, Cordie began to see the young man himself, sitting in a lawn chair outside with a parrot on his shoulder and another on his knee, speaking earnestly with them. Whenever the young man saw her, he would stop talking and wave. And as time passed, he was always there when Cordie ran.

In all of Cordie's short life as a runner, nothing had ever slowed her down. But the sight of the young man and his parrots came as close as anything ever would.

It is a common thing to fall in love with familiarity, to fall in love with something or someone who makes you feel safe simply because, every day, that something or someone never changes.

And so it was with the young man and his parrots and Cordie. Somehow, having never even met, the young man and Cordie fell in love. They fell in love with their familiarity. He sat outside with his parrots every day, she ran past him every day, they both loved everything about this every day, and they made their own story.

When Cordie died, quickly and surprisingly, without ever having even talked with the young man beside the running path, the story was left unfinished.

So Cordie is staying now in one of the small bed-and-breakfasts the Village reserves for its most temporary residents. The spirits living in the B&B's know for sure they aren't in the Village for long. They are really looking forward to heaven. Some can hardly wait. But each of them is like someone about to go on a trip who has to run back inside the house for one last thing.

For Cordie, the young man beside the river is the one last thing.

So every morning Cordie runs along the Village river and every evening she does the same. And as she runs, Cordie prays for the young man with his parrots. She prays that he will find love on the earth, that he will find work which fulfills him, that he will have good health and a long life, that he will always have parrots.

Cordie feels she cannot go on to the universe until she has sent back to earth blessings for someone important to her. This sort of thing happens in the Village a lot. One might expect that the blessings villagers send back would be to parents or close friends, children, brothers and sisters.

But sometimes it takes the journey to heaven for a person to realize how much others have meant. The kind grocer, the patient bus driver, the friendly little girl on the corner. These people would never guess that someone has stopped a few days in the Heavenly Village to bless and to pray for them. But often someone has.

Cordie loves her young man. And she is caring for him the best way she knows how: she is following the Village river with her runner's heart.

He hath made

everything beautiful

in its time.

ECCLESIASTES 3:11

*

The

Potter

IT IS WRITTEN that God created the earth in six days and six nights, and technically this is true, but He had actually been thinking about it long before that. This is the way of creation: like a seed in the ground, a tulip bulb in winter waiting for spring, creation comes first invisibly and settles quietly in the mind. It waits there. And when everything is right, when the heart is open and the mind free, a thing is made. In God's case, it was the earth. In the potter's case, it was a bowl.

The potter lives just at the edge of the Heavenly Village. His name is Thomas. He has a rather ramshackle little house that he uses for sleeping and eating, but his real home is his potter's shed in the backyard.

Walk in and there is nothing but soft clay dust everywhere. Everywhere! A potter's life is a messy one. There is the dust on the shelves, the wet mud on the floor, the ash of fire, the spill of glaze. Thomas loves music and he's tried three times to keep a tape player running in his shed. But it always gets clogged up with something.

Thomas is one of God's favorite people in the Heavenly Village. In fact, God asked Thomas if he would live there as a favor. Imagine God asking a person for a favor. But He did. God has admired the work of Thomas's hands for years. He has watched

Thomas from afar, sitting at his potter's wheel, pulling up a piece of moist clay into some exquisite vase or bowl or pitcher. God can't believe, sometimes, how similar He and Thomas are. How careful about craft. How devoted to creation. God watches Thomas throw a pot and He wonders if maybe He made the earth a little too fast. Maybe He should have taken more time. Worked the seventh day and rested the eighth.

God is inspired.

Thomas died when he was twenty-seven. It was a car accident. He hit his head and in an instant he was flying to heaven. Thomas had a few bowls he'd meant to glaze first, but other than that it was all right. He didn't mind returning to God.

But this time it was God Himself who wasn't so sure. God who saw Thomas on his way up and who looked behind at Thomas's silent potter's wheel on earth, at the clutter of creation in Thomas's shed that God had quietly lingered over, at the row of lovely pitchers just glazed in cobalt blue. God saw Thomas coming and realized maybe Thomas was ready for a change, but *He* wasn't.

He met Thomas at the door. This was unusual for God. Usually He sends a messenger angel or a loved one to meet a new spirit and welcome him home. God will embrace His child eventually, but He has learned that most people like to get a little unpacked, so to speak, before they meet the Creator.

Thomas didn't even get a chance to take his coat off. There was God in all His glory at heaven's front door. He had one of Thomas's pots in His hands. Thomas thought he'd sold that pot to a nice young woman at the county fair in Indiana. It just goes to show that God *is* everywhere.

God talked to the potter for a long time. He told Thomas how He loved the pureness of clay, the spell of the wheel, the strength and eternalness of the work. He told Thomas about His collection of pots. Some were thousands of years old, earth time. God told him that there is great wonder in heaven, but that He misses, sometimes, the humility of clay.

He asked if maybe Thomas could stop in the Heavenly Village and throw awhile. He said that there was a nice little ramshackle house with a potter's shed at the edge of town. (All of which God had rushed into being when He saw Thomas flying up.) He asked if Thomas might stay.

Well, who could deny God a favor? Of course Thomas said yes. But not just because God asked. Because Thomas thought it was a good idea. He died young. Maybe, through clay, he could finish his story.

He opened the door of the ramshackle house and invited God in for tea.

And theirs is one of the sweetest stories in the Heavenly Village.

All day long the villagers go about their

little tasks, their daily errands, their stories. They tidy their houses and clip their flowers and, now and again, make a quick run to the earth and back.

Then, around eleven o'clock every night, they all go to sleep.

All of them but one. He is out on the edge of town, just opening the door of his potter's shed and stepping inside. He is turning on the light and putting on his apron. He is ready to work.

Thomas's favorite time to work has always been during the dark hours past midnight. Interestingly, this has always been God's favorite time, too. It is well known that when He began creating the earth, the universe was completely black.

So it probably comes as no surprise that often, about 2 A.M., there is a knock on Thomas's door.

God is there, a bit shy about bothering

Thomas but wondering if He could step in. Thomas clears away the dust and offers Him a chair. God sits, with pleasure.

And there they are. The earth is turning below them like a child's favorite marble and stories are beginning and ending and beginning all over again.

Above them, stars are burning and a mystery is unfolding in the heavens. Angels sing.

And here in the Village, the peaceful spirits are sleeping safe in their beds, dreaming earthly dreams of vegetable gardens and friendly cats and warm cups of coffee at noon.

While they sleep, there is a steady sound, a constant hum, a soft flowing rhythm in the air. It comes from the edge of town. A young potter is placing God's hands on the wheel and the wheel is spinning round.

About this Scholastic Signature Author

CYNTHIA RYLANT grew up in a small town in West Virginia. Her first book, *When I Was Young in the Mountains*, was published in 1982 and named a Caldecott Honor Book. In the last two decades, Ms. Rylant has written numerous picture books, short stories, and novels, including *Missing May*, winner of the Newbery Medal. She currently lives in the Pacific Northwest.